the
nightmare
journal

by ekg

Hungry Goat Press
P.O. Box 806241
Saint Clair Shores, MI 48080
Attention Permissions Department

1st Edition
Hungry Goat Press is an Imprint of Gauthier Publications
www.EATaBOOK.com

ISBN: 978-1-942314-36-3

Hungry
Goat Press

to the therapist who assured me
writing them down would help the
nightmares stop...you never considered
they would appreciate the attention.

foreword

from the grotesque
from the insane
from the   unstable
from the deranged

from those who are feared
and those that you should
from those who are evil
masquerading as good

these words that follow
these words are theirs
read at your discretion
but be prepared

for the unsettling feeling
that becomes too much
the odd sensation
the phantom touch

the whispers that
from the darkness   prevail
the unexpected look
behind the   v eil

heed the warning
remember it well
as you walk slowly
through the gates of hell

never together
read only alone
each passage   singular
each one on its own

don't repeat the message
hidden in verse
this book is a nightmare

this book is a curse

heed the warning
remember it well
as you walk slowly
through the gates of hell

never together
read only alone
each passage   singular
each one on its own

don't repeat the message
hidden in verse
this book is a nightmare

this book is a curse

the sound

turning the corner, the darkened road
a faster way, or so you're told.
but the sky is bright, and you are brave
think of all the time you'll save.

just more dirt and a few more rocks
some dirty shoes and muddy socks.

so off you go into parts unknown
the other side, your beloved home.
nothing strange here to see
birds, flowers, the willow tree.

you like this way, the path is straight
closer to home, you won't be late.

the walk is easy, you're almost through
but then a feeling of eyes on you.
behind the bush or perhaps a tree
you look and look but do not see.

the path grows darker, the trees are
thick
you bend down, you grab a stick.
just a precaution, just in case
you continue on, a quickened   pace.

then you hear it, a delicate sound
it fills the air, you look around.
no one's there, no one you can see
just the woods, the   ancient tree.

soft as feathers, a child begins to sing
the voice gets loud, your ears do ring.
what sounded sweet has now turned
foul
the inaudible words more like a growl.

you walk faster, but the volume grows
beneath the tune, a murder of crows.
their cawing mimics the melody
you look up,   they fill the tree.

start to jog and then to run
in the distance a patch of sun.
but the farther you run, no closer you
get
a well-conceived trap, an invisible net.

by the time you realize your situation
the horrible truth, your desperation.
you've gone too far, no path in sight
it's not just dark,
it's almost night.

you continue on, stick in hand
ready now, but without a plan.
hours now, maybe days
time suspended in wooded haze.

you've escaped it finally, fall to the
ground
but soon again the beautiful, awful
sound.

looking around no one appears,
you unclasp your hands

you free your ears.

this time the song flows from your lips
foreign words against your fingertips.

close your mouth and hold it tight
until your teeth begin to bite.
but push down harder, it has to stop
nothing causes the volume to drop.

even as the skin dangles from your lips
your teeth are red, the blood it drips.

red tendrils trail down your hand
you're shaking now, can barely stand.
remove the demonic tune you must

your surroundings, yourself, you no
longer   trust.

your voice is screaming
your voice is strained.
high octaves your body cannot contain.

shouting still, you keep going
it's impossible but the volume is grow-
ing.

crimson blood fills your ears
diluted by the stream of tears.
and yet the pitch still is rising
your body begins compromising.

the note at its highest,
causing your bones to crack
your hands, your legs, and then your
back.

the words too soft to hear so you strain
below the delicate notes, a cry of pain.

you can hear it clearly now, and in
vain
the sound repeating is
                          your name.

shh...now you've heard it
before,
that soft little tapping on your
door.
straining to hear the tiny sound,
it knows you're listening and

begins
to
pound.

hide and seek

you lock the door, you hide the key
you put it where no one will see

it's not a crime it's not a sin
it was their fault that they went in

the room was empty, or so it would
seem
you knew better, you had the dream

you didn't know that when you came
ready to play their silly game

into the house for hide and seek
count to fifty, never peek.

but the walls were too familiar for you
you knew what doors to go through

deja vu   and nothing more
you tell yourself as you explore

looking for a hiding place
to win the game, to save face

you're braver than them all you said
if you don't leave now, you'll
be dead

just a dream, nothing more
you tell yourself when you find the
drawer

in the bedroom across the hall
you reach inside to find the doll

her porcelain face blackened with age
against the wall, the victorian cage

inside, the bird just like your dream
it's only bones but starts to scream

find your friends, leave the place
you begin to panic, your heart to race

it's just a house and nothing more
you tell yourself when you find the door

you know what horror lays inside
of course in there, they would hide

the room calls as it always did
should have been more careful where
they hid

but this is no nightmare, you have a
choice   you hear a changing in their
voice

looking down you see the lock
you find the key behind the clock

slide and turn until the tumblers click
you feel sorry,   you feel sick

as their giggles turn to screams
you don't need to see, you've had the
dreams

the events happening behind the door
you have been there many times before

fists bang against the wood
you wish you could tell them it does no
good

silly for them to try and fight

perhaps you will
                    sleep tonight

the house

the house is there
yet nowhere it seems
consuming the night
engulfing my dreams

a mimic
     a copy
a demented twist
reality soured
yet it must exist

every night i wake inside
always running
trying to hide

there is no address
no direction
no map
i'm always there
i can't get back

every night a little longer
every sensation a little stronger
walls once bare now pictures hold
putrid and worn   impossibly cold

i know the landscape
i know the ground
yet the house cannot be found

threats unknowable
but known still
the house is deadly
the house   can kill

        or maybe it's
so much
so much worse
maybe not death
but an eternal curse

everynight a labrynth unfolds
looking for victims
hungry for souls

in a decaying fortress
that hides in a dream
disguised as a nightmare
that wakes with a scream

until dream and reality one day merge
until fear and anticipation finally con-
verge

find it one day no doubt i have
on the storming night
i'll go stark raving mad

i'll look in the window
as i have before
there's a girl inside
running towards the door.

away from the towering shadow
with no features to see
i'll understand then that
the   girl   is   me.

the fall

when you awake you won't recall
the inevitable drop. the terrible fall

you'll feel tired. this is true
that's the only effect it will have on
you

of course, there's only
so many falls you can make
only so many your mind can take

think twice before you sleep
or the bad thoughts will come. they'll
creep

then you find yourself on a ledge
you're looking down from the edge

those bad thoughts have come alive
you can't take it so you dive

the fall is hard, the fall is fast
you see images from your past

so much regret, you close your eyes
trying to forget your terrible lies

your silent screams, i can hear
the air is thick with the smell of fear

you wake up covered in sweat
a glimpse of images,   then you for-
get

arms open,
              at the bottom   i   wait
you come so close, but it's too late

it's just a dream, it can't be true
don't worry child,

              i'll be seeing you

jar of lies

my little jar of lies tucked neatly by
my bed
all the horrible deeds and acts
nestled snug under my head.

one i have yet to add
                        one that's left to do
you have yet to realize

it's what i have

            done to you.

the fountain

careful the coin inside you place,
let not the statues see your   face.
what is beautiful and safe by day,
turns to horror
                        as night gives way.

the statues cast, a forgotton lore
a terrible truth,   a hidden door.
the man behind it's creation knew,
unearthly things, terrible and true.

their cherub faces grow grotesque at
night,   summon the monsters that
plague this site.
so beware those among these cobblestone
          tread.
with a quickened pace you should have
fled.

drop nothing, leave nothing behind.
or come into your home, you they will
find.
run along now, go away.
in this place

                        you are not safe to stay.

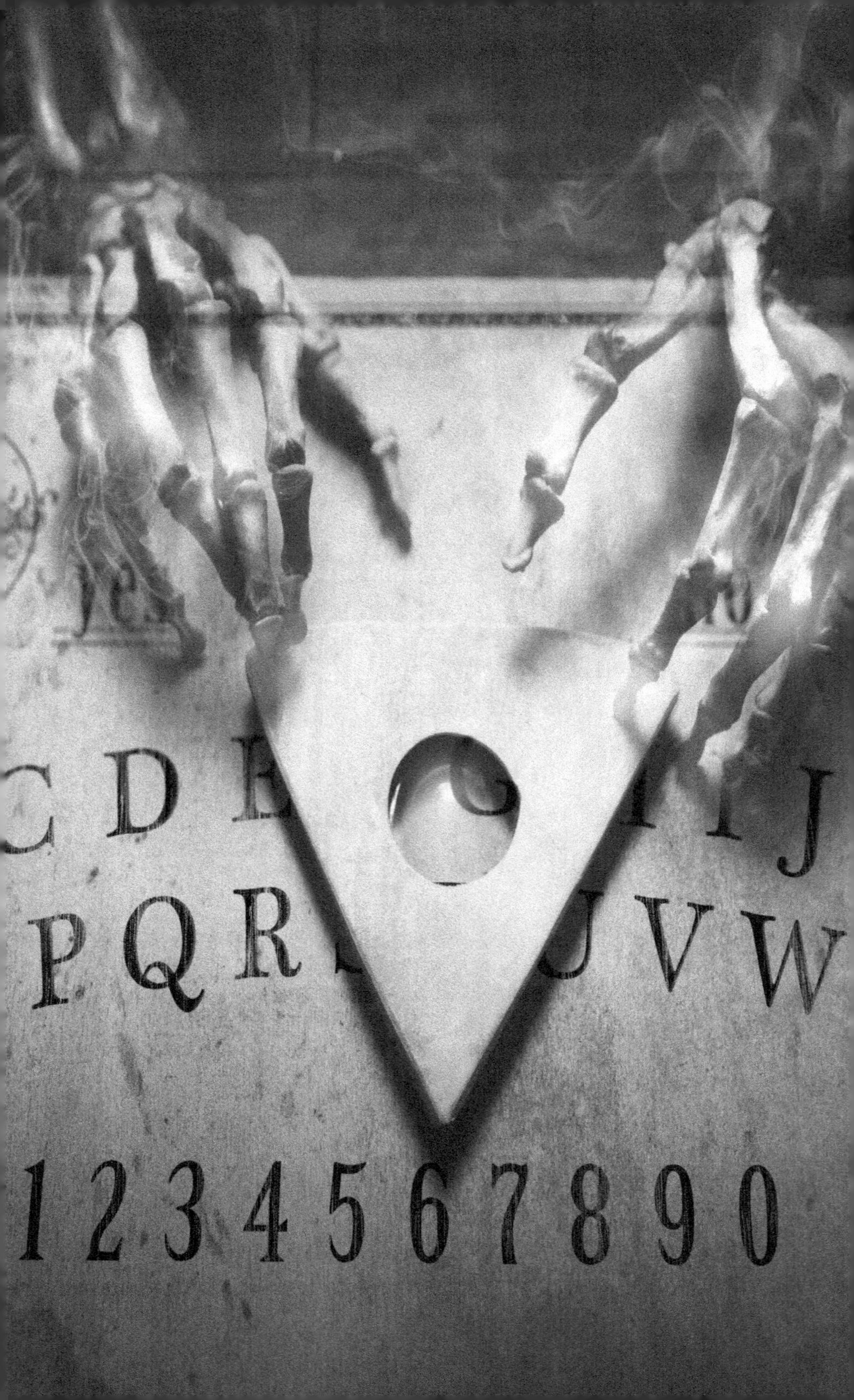
C D E
I J
P Q R
U V W
1 2 3 4 5 6 7 8 9 0

the game

only wood and nothing more
after all   you've done this before

fingertips only.   you know how to play
have ready the question you want to say

don't shift your fingers. it begins to move
across the wood silent and smooth

letters magnified. candles burn
you wait quietly it's almost your turn

more letters. faster now
a bead of sweat drips from your
brow

a silent chuckle. a lower hum
no way to know where it's coming from

your friends gone. you're all alone
you share the planchette with hands of
bone

don't worry when it spells out your name
remember child.

                        it's just a game

cursed ship

a   small box, a tiny gift
long ago set adrift
upon the wild and crashing waves
as the passengers fell to their graves

no known cause, just a tale
of ghost and demons setting sail

once upon a time,
as so many stories do
this one however is   dark
horrifying   but true

the ship itself a massive beast
crossing monthly west to east
a single maiden,
a perilous cry
             she boarded the ship
they believed the lie

long blonde tresses, soft pale skin
unable to see what was within

she was their angel
           the sailors fell in love
she 'd come to them from up above

she sang and danced against the rail
waving out at the ocean
she began to wail

banshee was she, this they knew
sailors covered their ears
but her song came through

the sailors fell in love with her voice
the hypnotic octave left little choice

attack one another they did
except one small   boy who ran
and hid

years now since he heard a sound
since his father struck him to the ground
he could see the men argue and riot
but in his world
                        all was quiet

there she stood on the bow
dancing around smiling now

 a siren, a demon, something even worse
upon the ship she brought a curse

the men, once brothers,
tearing each other apart

she had them now'

she owned their heart
        when all went quiet

the sailors fell dead
the young boy sat there
filled with dread

the nymph looked over and saw the boy
grinning wide a smile of joy
she raised a hand waived goodbye
into the sea

        with a banshee cry.

told by the fire

a friendly stranger.
a kind smile.
why would it matter if he stayed awhile?

long enough to weave the tale.
full of clues and a hidden trail.

the story full of excitement and legend
abound.
a treasure just waiting to be found.
not believing but you went all the same.
an adventurous afternoon, a fun little
game.

find the entrance in its hiding place.
a grin forming on your face.
as your feet walk on the cursed ground.
you only think of fortune found.

you broke the ground.
ignored the sign.
removed the contents.
left nothing behind.

but you weren't the first to find this
space.
where horrid things had taken place.
a guide of sorts perhaps was he.
waiting there behind the tree.

for another group perhaps even now.
to tell the tale with furrowed brow.

damned the dirt beneath your feet.
as you walk in the opening, you should
retreat.
but forward you move when the last clue
found.
break the dirt. disturb ground.

your flashlight went dark,
you remember now.
if you had only known somehow.

the twisted legend. the trap in place.
that no one ever had left this space

their bones around you.
scratches along the wall.
some of them over nine feet tall.

you mumble things. plead your case.
to the grotesque and monstrous   face.
close your eyes tight and begin to
cry.
whispering now

                    the last goodbye.

the debt

i'm not afraid i'm not afraid
it's just a debt   it must be paid

find the stone
wait for the eclipse
whisper the words upon my lips

500 years ago the pact was made
the blood was spilled
the foundation laid

clench my fist   hold on tight
i've waited my life for tonight

be brave
be brave
see it through
   everyone's lives count on you

upon the pale lit shore, came a man with
little more
than a soft tap upon the ground no road
behind him just the sound

lighting strikes, a clap of thunder
a cloud of fog rolled from
                              under

no one to witness the shadow figure but i
and the faded stars up in the sky
standing taller than a man should
in his hands a   box of wood.

approached me on that distant shore
his features now clearer   than before
black as night his cloak and hat
walking beside him, an ebony cat

the smoke that trails around his feet
spun and twirled as we did meet
i could not run or turn away
from the strange figure and his display

below the brim a face did show
his eyes ablaze with unearthly glow
  his face transformed before i could flee
the world became too dark to see

the box was open, i knew this much
  as my fingers reached out to touch
the thing inside i could not understand
reaching out an icy hand

the last flash i recall
his face became mine,   and that is
all.

there is a house
it's not your home
there you sit
you're all alone

the sun shines in
the door is locked
you can't see out
the windows blocked

the walls once tall
start to shrink
your eyes are dry
you cannot blink

the ceilings close
there's no room
a fitting place
an unhappy tomb

the show

a nightmare from which you can't awaken
should have thought twice before the pills
were   taken

but down they went and you waited
the affects of it anticipated

a strange taste, an odd sensation
not the usual hallucination

something's wrong, not right at all
the ground gives out you begin to fall

a bad batch, you'll just wait it out
nothing to go and panic about

you've done his before,you know how to
cope
you look down
you're holding a rope

where did it come from?
you don't know
you see it now
you're in the show

dozens of eyes fixed on you
you're not sure what you should do

a strange stage
lights shining bright
unable to tell   if it's day or night

props around you,
some sort of act
you pick them up
you put them back

selecting items you begin to juggle
it's easy for you
no sign of struggle

not sure how you know to do it
just focusing
just get through it

for the rope they let out a cheer
you twirl it around
like you're lassoing
  steer

a few tricks now, jump in and out
they love it, then stand
they scream, they shout

half the room light, the other dark
you hear a noise
you see a spark
flames around you and they grow

the audience cheers
their   eyes aglow

you see nothing
just orange and red
hear some shouts
but not what is said

you notice a door as it appears
you run away
control your fears

you know this room
the one you're in
it's where the   nightmare did begin

you see now yourself suspended
your neck broken
your life has ended

but there you sit rope in hand
beginning now to   understand

behind you they cheer as they're coming
it is futile,
              no use in   running